SHERMAN IS A SLOWPOKE

By Mitchell Sharmat

Illustrated by David Neuhaus

SCHOLASTIC INC. / New York

Library of Congress Cataloging-in-Publication Data
Sharmat, Mitchell.
Sherman is a slowpoke
Summary: A slow sloth decides to go to school to
learn how to think.
[1. Sloths—Fiction.   2. Schools—Fiction]
I. Neuhaus, David, ill.   II. Title.
PZ7.S52992Sh   1988   [E]   87-12746
ISBN 0-590-40938-7

12 11 10 9 8 7 6 5 4 3 2 1   8 9/8 0 1 2 3/9

Printed in the U.S.A.   23

FIRST SCHOLASTIC PRINTING, APRIL 1988

For Dad, who said, "TRY!"
—M.S.

For Jared, Lisa, Jenny,
and Christian.
—D.N.

Sherman was a giant sloth.

He lived with his mother and father at the bottom of a large tree in a forest.

Like all sloths, Sherman was slow at everything he did.

Even when he ate. And Sherman loved to eat.

A good meal could take him days.

But even more than eating, Sherman loved to sleep.

He could sleep all day, all night, all week.

One night Sherman and his father and mother had just finished eating.

"Burp," said his father, and he closed his eyes.

"Burp," said his mother, and she closed her eyes.

"Burp burp."

Sherman looked up. In front of him was the prettiest
sloth he had ever seen.
"I'm Sherman Sloth," said Sherman. "Who are you?"
"I'm Sheila," she said.

"Where are you going?" asked Sherman.

"To school," said Sheila.

"You go to school at night?" asked Sherman.

"Of course not, silly," said Sheila.

"School doesn't start until morning. I'm getting an
early start because I'm so slow."

"That sounds like a lot of trouble to me," said Sherman.

"It's worth it," said Sheila. "I'm learning how to do
things and how to think."

"Now look who is silly," said Sherman. "Everyone knows
that sloths don't *do* and sloths don't *think*."

"That's not true," said Sheila. "I know some things
that even *you* can do."

Sherman got interested.
"Like what?" he asked.
"Like eating and sleeping. I can see just by looking at
you that you do them very well."
Sherman felt proud.

"And what about thinking?" asked Sherman.
"Try it," said Sheila. "There's a first time for everything."
Sherman tried and tried, but he could not get a thought.
All he got was dizzy, so he yawned and fell asleep.
Sheila crawled off into the night.

The next morning Sherman's family was having breakfast.
Sherman sighed.
"What's the matter?" yawned his mother.
"I'm not happy," he said. "I've spent my whole life near
this tree. And all I do is eat and sleep."
"Sloths are always happy," said his father, "as long as
the leaves are green and the water is clean."
"I want more," said Sherman.

"I want to do things. I want to think. *I want to go to school!*"

"Do? Think? School?" said his mother.

"Out of the question!" said his father. "Sloths don't go to school."

"But times are changing," said Sherman.

"Sloths don't change," said his father, and he closed his eyes and went to sleep.

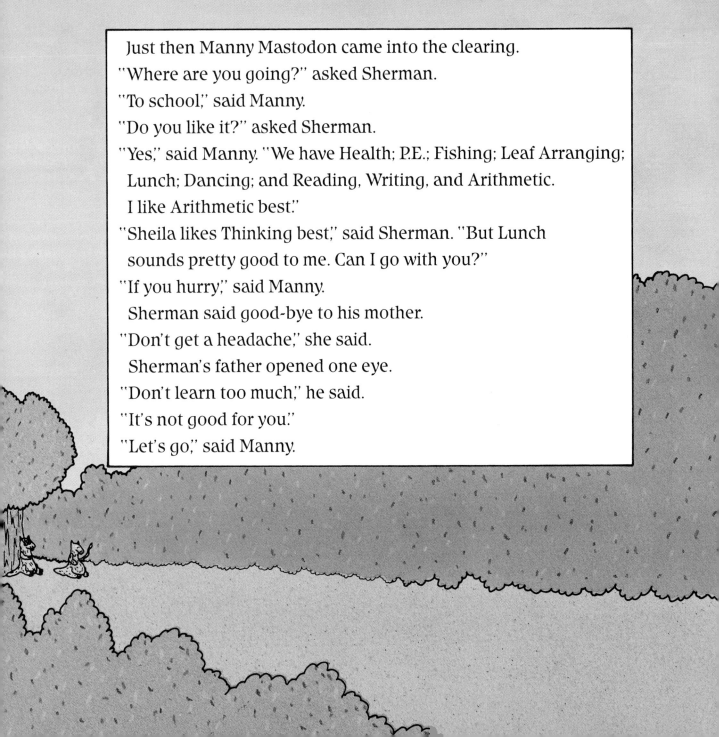

Just then Manny Mastodon came into the clearing.

"Where are you going?" asked Sherman.

"To school," said Manny.

"Do you like it?" asked Sherman.

"Yes," said Manny. "We have Health; P.E.; Fishing; Leaf Arranging; Lunch; Dancing; and Reading, Writing, and Arithmetic. I like Arithmetic best."

"Sheila likes Thinking best," said Sherman. "But Lunch sounds pretty good to me. Can I go with you?"

"If you hurry," said Manny.

Sherman said good-bye to his mother.

"Don't get a headache," she said.

Sherman's father opened one eye.

"Don't learn too much," he said.

"It's not good for you."

"Let's go," said Manny.

Sherman dragged himself off into the forest.

"Faster, Sherman!" said Manny.

"I'm dragging as fast as I can," gasped Sherman.

"I'll push you," said Manny.

He got behind Sherman and pushed.

"Ouch!" said Sherman.

"Your tusks are too sharp!"

Sherman picked a leaf and sat down.

"Now what?" Manny asked.

"It must be time for lunch," said Sherman.

"You're impossible and I'm late," said Manny.

And he ran off, muttering, "Sherman is a slowpoke."

Sherman ate the leaf and a small bush. Then he went to sleep under a giant fern.

When he awoke, Sheila was sitting beside him under the fern.

"What are you doing so far from home?" she asked.

"I'm on my way to school," said Sherman.

"School is over for today," said Sheila, "but if you keep going now, you should be on time for tomorrow."

"Will you go with me?" asked Sherman.

"Sure," said Sheila.

Sherman picked two leaves and gave one to Sheila.

"What a tasty snack," she said.

Sherman and Sheila walked and ate their way through the night.

"You got here at last," Manny said to Sherman at
school the next morning.
"Meet your classmates," said Sheila.
"Alice Alligator, Ringo Rhinoceros, Boris Bear,
Sammy Saber-toothed Tiger, Ellie Elephant, and Dawn Horse.
And this is Mr. Mammoth, our teacher."

"What brings you to school, Sherman?" asked Mr. Mammoth.
"I want to learn to think," said Sherman.
"That's what school is all about," said Mr. Mammoth.
"But your first lesson will be Health. You must get
rid of all that mud and green mold. Here is a bath
brush and there is the river. Rub and scrub."

Sherman sighed, took the bath brush, and walked into the river.

He sat down and started to fall asleep.

"Wake up! Wake up!" shouted Alice Alligator, and she splashed Sherman with her tail.

"Enough! Enough!" Sherman shouted, and he started to take his bath.

Sherman had never worked so long and so hard in his whole life. He scrubbed all twenty feet of himself. Mr. Mammoth came over and looked at Sherman. "You've washed off the mud," he said, "but the green mold is still all over you."

"I can't help it," said Sherman. "It grows back as fast as I wash it off. I'm pooped."

"I see," said Mr. Mammoth. He helped Sherman back to shore and propped him up against a tree.

Sherman fell asleep and began to snore.

Sammy Saber-toothed Tiger roared at Sherman.

Alice Alligator bit Sherman's tail.

Ellie Elephant shook Sherman.

Sherman just slept on.

Finally Mr. Mammoth poured a trunkful of water on Sherman's face.

"What's the matter?" sputtered Sherman.

"You've been sleeping and snoring in class," said Mr. Mammoth.

"But I need my sleep," said Sherman.

"Sherman," Mr. Mammoth said, "what you need is exercise. It's time for P.E."

"Sloths don't do P.E.," said Sherman.

"They do in this school," said Mr. Mammoth.

"Now you run up and down with Ringo Rhinoceros.
On your mark, get set, go!"

Ringo took off with Sherman following as fast as he could.
Sherman ran and ran until he was out of breath.
He ran until he cracked his head on the first large
tree he came to.

"Ouch!" said Sherman, and he sat down.

"This is hopeless, my head hurts. My chest aches.
My legs are weak and wobbly. And I haven't had
one thought all day."

"What *have* you learned?" asked Mr. Mammoth.

"I learned to wash off mud," said Sherman.

"I learned that my green mold grows as fast as I can
wash it off. I learned to run very slowly.
And I learned to do without lunch."

"That's not bad for a start," said Mr. Mammoth.

Mr. Mammoth spoke to the class, "It's time for Arithmetic."
He held up two large leaves.
"I have one leaf in my right hand and one leaf in my
left hand," he said. "How many leaves do I have in all?"
"Two," said Ringo.
"Two!" shouted Sammy.
"And what do you say, Sherman?" asked Mr. Mammoth.
"Enough for a good snack to share with one friend
under a fern," Sherman said.
Mr. Mammoth smiled. "That's a nice thought."
"Oh, Sherman," said Sheila, "you had a thought!"
"I did? I did!" Sherman exclaimed. "Hooray!"
Sherman jumped up and down. Then he stopped.
"I just thought," he said. "I must have been thinking
all my life."
"Of course you have," said Mr. Mammoth.

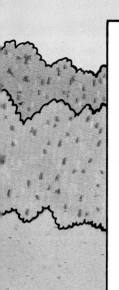

"We can do *that*," said Sherman's father.
And they all danced the Sloth Drag until the moon came up.